For Debbie Marten
J.W.

For my Jenna
J.

First published in 2015 by Nosy Crow Ltd
The Crow's Nest, 10a Lant Street
London SE1 1QR
www.nosycrow.com

ISBN 978 0 85763 492 4 (HB)
ISBN 978 0 85763 493 1 (PB)

A CIP catalogue record for this book is available from the British Library.

Printed in China by Imago

Papers used by Nosy Crow are made from wood grown in sustainable forests.

1 3 5 7 9 8 6 4 2 (HB)
1 3 5 7 9 8 6 4 2 (PB)

PoLES APaRT

Jeanne Willis

Illustrated by Jarvis

WORLD MAP

nosy crow

As everyone knows,
penguins are found at the South Pole
and never at the North Pole.

At least, not until the day . . .

. . . the Pilchard-Browns got lost on their way to a picnic.

Mr Pilchard-Brown was in charge of the map.

He told everyone to turn **right** at the snowman.

Which was **wrong**.

Now here they all were, on the other side
of the world – Mr and Mrs Pilchard-Brown,
Peeky, Poots and Pog . . .

. . . drifting towards an **enormous**, furry, white . . .

. . . something.

"Is it a lion? Is it a tiger?" asked Peeky and Poots.

"Is it a picnic blanket?" asked Pog.

The enormous something looked them up and down.

He had never seen anything like the Pilchard-Browns before.

"I'm Mr White," he said.

"I'm a polar bear, and you are?"

"Parrots!" said Peeky and Poots.

"Pork pies!" said Pog.

"We're penguins," said Mrs Pilchard-Brown.

"What are you doing here?" wondered Mr White.

"This is where polar bears live, **not** penguins."

"We're going to a picnic at the South Pole," said Pog.

"This is the **North Pole,** my friends," said Mr White.

"The South Pole is **12,430** miles *that* way."

"So, I was a few miles out," shrugged Mr Pilchard-Brown.

"Anyone can make a mistake."

"Don't think of it as a mistake," said Mr White.
"Think of it as a **big adventure**.
I have often dreamt of being the first polar bear
to reach the South Pole . . ."

"Mummy says we should always follow our dreams," said Peeky.
"Daddy says we should always follow him," said Poots.
"Lead the way, Mr White," said Mrs Pilchard-Brown.

The penguins followed Mr White
over land and sea.

"Eek!" said Peeky.

"Whoa!" said Poots.

"Can we have our picnic now?" said Pog.
But it wasn't the best spot,
so they followed Mr White
all the way to . . .

. . . America.

"Howdy!" said Mr Pilchard-Brown.

"Busy!" said Peeky.

"Buzzing!" said Poots.

"Can we have our picnic?" said Pog.
"Not now, dear," said Mrs Pilchard-Brown.

5TH AVE

America was **awesome**
but it wasn't home, so they followed
Mr White all the way to . . .

. . . England.

"How do you do?"
said Mr Pilchard-Brown.

"Grey!" said Peeky.

"Grand!" said Poots.

"Can we have our picnic?" said Pog.
"Not now, dear," said Mrs Pilchard-Brown.
England was charming but it wasn't home,
so they followed Mr White all the way to . . .

. . . Italy.

"Ciao!" said Mr Pilchard-Brown.

"Wet!" said Peeky.

"Wonderful!" said Poots.

"I need a wee," said Pog.
"Not in there, dear,"
said Mrs Pilchard-Brown.

Italy was magnifico but it wasn't home,

so they followed Mr White all the way to . . .

. . . India.

"Namaste!"
said Mr Pilchard-Brown.

"Hot!" said Peeky.

"Huge!" said Poots.

"Put the python down, dear,"
said Mrs Pilchard-Brown.

India was **dazzling**
but it wasn't home, so
they followed Mr White
all the way to . . .

. . . Australia.

"G'day!" said Mr Pilchard-Brown.

"Faster!" said Peeky.

"Fun!" said Poots.

"Can we have our picnic now?" said Pog.
"Soon," said Mrs Pilchard-Brown.

Australia was **bonzer** but it still wasn't home,
so they followed Mr White . . .

. . . over the land and over the sea.
On and on they went.

But of all the wonderful places in the world,
there was no place like home.
"Are we nearly there yet?"
said Peeky, Poots and Pog.

"It's not far now," said Mr White
and they followed him left, right,

left, right,

all the way . . .

. . . home!

"Please stay, Mr White," said Peeky and Poots.

"You can share our picnic," said Pog.

So Mr White stayed and, for a while, he was happy.

But the South Pole wasn't his home.
He was a polar bear
and polar bears don't live there.

Which is why he said goodbye and
walked 12,430 miles all the way back to . . .

. . . the North Pole,

where he belonged.

He'd followed his **wildest** dream and had
the **best** adventure. Even so, he was sad to think
that he would **never** see a penguin again.

But to Mr White's delight . . .

. . . he did!

"Hello, how did you get there?" he said.

"Where is your family?"

"Here we are!"
said Mr Pilchard-Brown.

"Someone put my egg in your hat,"
said Mrs Pilchard-Brown.

Peeky and Poots pointed at Pog.

"Can we have our picnic now?" he said.

And although the North Pole
isn't home to penguins, Mr White was
always happy to see friends.

"Welcome back!" he said.